#39751

Davis, Lee
P. B. Bear: Catch that
hat!

E
D

A DK Publishing Book

Senior Designer   Claire Jones
Senior Editor   Caryn Jenner
Editor   Fiona Munro
US Editor   Kristin Ward
Production   Katy Holmes
Photography   Dave King

First American Edition, 1997
2 4 6 8 10 9 7 5 3 1

Published in the United States by
DK Publishing, Inc.
95 Madison Avenue
New York, New York 10016

Visit us on the World Wide Web at: http://www.dk.com

ISBN 0-7894-1413-9

Reproduced in Italy by G.R.B. Graphica, Verona
Printed and bound in Italy by L.E.G.O.

Acknowledgments
DK would like the thank the following manufacturers
for permission to photograph copyright material:
D.S. Nicholass Limited for the toy pig
Folkmanis, Inc. for the toy hen puppet

DK would also like to thank
Barbara Owen, Vera Jones, Robert Fraser and Dave King
for their help with props and set design.

38751

Can you find
the little bear
in each scene?

P.B. BEAR

Catch That Hat!

Lee Davis

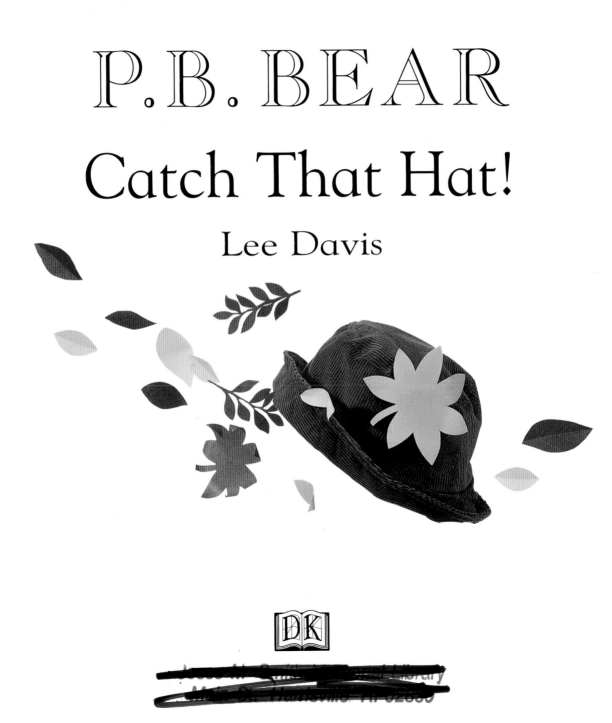

DK

It was a windy fall day.
As P.B. Bear stepped out of his house,
he saw leaves swirling down from the trees.

There were yellow leaves   ,

red leaves   , orange leaves   ,

and brown leaves   .

Crinkle, crackle, crunch, scrunch
went the leaves under his feet.

P.B. Bear's friends waved to him from the gate.
"I like your new blue hat," said Patsy the pig.
"Thank you," said P.B. "It keeps
the wind out of my ears."
"We've come to play with you,"
said Hilda the hen.
"Let's play in the leaves!"
laughed P.B.
Patsy and Hilda went
through the gate and
into the yard.

P.B. gathered a pile of leaves in his arms.
"Look!" he called, as he threw them into the air.
Patsy and Hilda watched the leaves float down
to the ground.
"I can do that!" said Patsy.
"Me, too!" said Hilda.
The three friends gathered a pile of leaves, then —
"1, 2, 3!" shouted P.B.
All together, they threw the leaves into the air.

WHOOOOOSSSSHHH!
A gust of wind whistled through the trees
and blew the leaves away.
"Hold on to your hat, P.B. Bear!" called Patsy.

WHOOOOOSSSSHHH!
It was too late.
Another gust of wind lifted P.B.'s hat
off his head and into the air.
"Stop!" called P.B. "That's my hat!"
But the wind blew the hat higher and higher.
"Oh, no!" said P.B. "Catch that hat!"

The hat blew into a tree.
"We'll never catch my hat now,"
sighed P.B. Bear.
"Don't worry," said Hilda. "I'll get it."
Up she went, flapping her wings
until she landed in the tree.
But just as Hilda reached out for the hat —
WHOOOOOSSSSHHH!
Another gust of wind blew it away!

"There it goes!" called Patsy.
Crinkle, crackle, crunch, scrunch
went the leaves as she chased
P.B. Bear's hat across the yard.
At last the hat floated down to the ground.
But just as Patsy reached out to grab it —
WHOOOOOSSSSHHH!
Another gust of wind blew the hat away!

"Come back, hat!" called P.B.

WHOOOOOSSSSHHH!

P.B. looked around the yard,
but he couldn't see his hat.
"Where are you, hat?" he wondered.
At last, he spotted it.
He crawled into the pile of leaves.
They crinkled and crackled
and crunched and scrunched
all around him.

P.B. jumped out of the pile of leaves.

Crinkle, crackle, crunch, scrunch.

"Look! Here's my hat!" he said.

"Hooray!" cheered Hilda and Patsy.

"We all helped catch my hat," said P.B.

"We make a good team."

The three friends gathered up some leaves.

"Ready?" shouted P.B. "1, 2, 3!"

Together, they threw the leaves into the air.

At that moment —

WHOOOOOSSSSHHH!

went the wind,

and blew the leaves away.

But this time P.B. Bear held

his hat safely in his paw.